TRUISM

TRUISM

Carolyn Nelson

Truism

First published January 2017 by Black Jack Books

© Carolyn Nelson

All rights reserved

Illustrations from Pixabay.com, used with permission.

ISBN 978-0-9944802-1-7

Black Jack Books

To my beautiful sister, Yolande,
For her guidance and inspiration.

And to Valerie Goodreid, without whom,
The blind man's voice would never have been heard.

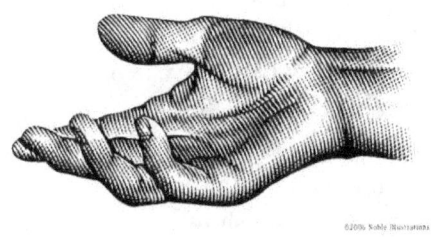

"Come take my hand," the blind man said,
"And I'll open up your eyes."
His voice, just like a tolling bell,
Heard above the hawker's cries.
He was standing by the fountain
In the crowded village square,
So intent upon their business
Few had noticed he was there.

Much like any other village,
With its masters and its slaves,
And the poor, whose heavy burdens
Took them early to their graves.
Insulated in their thinking,
Plodding in a stagnant groove,
Many spouting their conviction
There was nothing they need prove.
But he could not be discouraged,
As his patience was his creed,
While leaning on his walking staff
He reached out to those in need.

1

Other senses had been heightened
As his sight began to fade,
Through nose and ears, his tongue and skin,
He saw more than eyes displayed.
He heard the clink of manacles,
Tasted metal on his tongue,
Echoed pain had gripped his ankles
From scars earned when he was young.
Why that memory had surfaced
He was at a loss to know,
But in keeping with his training
He would wait for it to show.

"Come take my hand," he said again,
"And your vision I will clear."
Though the crowd began dispersing,
A few had remained quite near.
Not close enough to take his hand
But to hear the old man speak,
He said, "The mind can free the blind
And provide the sight you seek."

"I find your words most confusing,"
Said a man who stood nearby
"But I've time to stay and listen
To your entertaining lie.
By what means will you enrich us
From your wealth of poverty?
What great wisdom can you offer
With your sad deformity?"
The blind man smiled a knowing smile
At the man who seemed so sure,
With his condescending manner
He had met his kind before.

"If you're inclined, then sit awhile
And my meaning I'll make clear,
I am blind through loss of eyesight,
Not through ignorance or fear."

The man reacted in offence,
Thought some insult had been paid
But he made himself look foolish
With the anger he displayed.
"I am a most important man,
No-one speaks to me that way."
But he made a hasty exit
When he heard the old man say…

"There is no strength in violence,
Anger holds no dignity
And abuse shows only weakness
In the vain and cowardly."

"Come take my hand," the old man said,
"And I'll open up your eyes
But I hereby warn the pompous
I will cut you down to size!"
And as they had seen him do this
They did not dispute he would,
As two more left the village square
Only ten now sat or stood.
The power they heard in his voice
Made the villagers unsure,
He changed his tone to one more kind
As he sought to reassure.

He smiled and said, "Come take my hand
And your vision I will clear."
Then he spoke to boost the courage

Of the one he heard, draw near.
"What I offer you is knowledge,
Do not fear the face of truth,
It was a constant source of joy
And excitement in your youth."
Her hand was placed inside his own
He was grateful for her trust,
Through the contact, he gained insight
To best serve her… as he must.
At her touch his vision altered,
The scars tightened on his back,
As he wondered if hers also
Looked like lines drawn on a map.

Sending warmth down through his fingers
He began to ease her mind,
To keep her open to his words
Which at first, could sound unkind.

"Though you're bound to many people,
In your heart, you feel alone,
You live within a circumstance
And its making is your own.
To see how you have reached this place…
Ask yourself… what makes you cry?
Then look for things that make you laugh,
You can find them if you try.
If the sadness outweighs laughter
Your beliefs may be unsound,
This can hold you in the shadows
Where your doubts and fears abound.
It distorts your understanding
Making your life seem unfair…
This can build up to self-pity
So, I warn you to beware!

The lost will want to make you lost
And the low, to bring you low
But if you choose to fail yourself
You will reap all that you sow."

"Now open up your eyes," he said
"See you've earned all that you own
But you can change your circumstance
If you trust in what you're shown.
Believing you can't change your life
Is the only real mistake,
And giving yourself bad advice
Is a habit you can break.

Just think about those special times
When you felt yourself worthwhile,
That gave you pride and confidence,
Warmed your spirit with a smile.
Now hold on tight to feeling good,
Let the rightness fill your mind,
To care for you and keep you safe
Be the friend you need to find."

He then released her from his grip
With just one thing left to say
"What you believe, is what you are
And what you invite your way."

"I'll speak more kindly to myself,
Try to keep my spirits high
And aim to be my own best friend,"
This she swore, then said, "Goodbye."

As she left, he knew his wisdom
Was not wasted on her youth,

Because inside her troubled mind
He had placed the seed of truth.

*

"Come take my hand," the blind man said,
"And I'll open up your eyes."
He waited there with outstretched hand
For the next to free from lies.

The courage of the one so young
Made another woman brave,
The old man's heart swelled up with pride
For the soul that he might save.
The adult female took his hand,
She felt lost and so confused,
The blind man said, "Your mind is fogged
By a life-skill you've not used."
He knew she didn't understand
So, he spoke to reassure,
Saying, "It's just information
That you didn't have before.

When you're pressured to compliance
You do not need to obey
Nor sacrifice your own free will
To do what some others say.
What two choices you are offered
You are not restricted to,
With some thought, you'll find your third choice,
One of benefit to you!
Being hampered and restricted
For a lifetime… takes a toll,
But once you claim your right to choose
You will then gain **self-control**.

You will not be obligated
To let others have their way,
As no-one else can take from you
What you will not give away!
That's the beauty of all errors,
Once they're seen... they can be cured,
Just by breaking a bad habit
A life skill is your reward."

Her hand was still held in his own
When she said... "Just a mistake...
That somehow I have never known
My third choice is mine to make!"
He felt the tension leave her grip
As she claimed her own free will
And breathed in her own three choices
Saying... "**This is my life skill**."

Somehow, she forgot to thank him
But that never was his need,
He heard the firmness in her step
And knew he had sown a seed.

*

"Come take my hand," the blind man said
"And your vision I will clear."
He felt his attention sharpen
And his first thoughts reappear.

A step... a tap, a step... a tap
First a foot and then a crutch,
The blind man braced his tender heart
For the feel of sorrows' touch.
As the old man took the boy's hand

For a moment, they were one,
The same shackles bound their ankles
But the harm could be undone.
The boy's body had been broken
But he wasn't ruled by fear,
The blind man paused to clear his mind,
Pity served no purpose here.

Through his gift, he healed wrong thinking,
Giving healthy thoughts instead,
Planting one more seed of wisdom
Was his goal and so he said…
"If you focus on unkindness
That is all you'll ever see,
By losing sight of what is good
You're inviting misery.
Although evil is not treasure
And should not be seen as such,
There is still a wealth of knowledge
Found in each inhuman touch.
You have gained some precognition
And no longer need to fear
As your skin is sure to prickle
Every time that evil's near.
Don't waste time on seeking answers
To what cruel minds have done,
You could never think as they do
For you are the healthy one.
And although it may surprise you
You are very lucky too
Just because you're not infected
By the evil they showed you.
You can learn and grow… develop,
You can choose to change your mind,
You can care for others' feelings,

Which is quite beyond their kind.
And you have a secret weapon,
You can nullify their wrongs
By confining your reaction
To the past... where it belongs.
You are strong of mind and purpose
Not the victim of their plan,
You'll become older and wiser,
The true measure of a man."

"I do thank you for your guidance
And I promise I will try
To fulfil my true potential"
This he swore, then said, "Goodbye."

The old man had many virtues,
Seeds of truth he used as tools,
He was patient and kind hearted
But he seldom suffered fools.
Still he waited... ever hopeful...
Always offering his hand
To the one who had the courage
And the will to understand.

"Come take my hand," the blind man said
Hoping one more would submit...
**"Why have a life experience?
If there's nothing learned from it!"**

*

The sun had set... the crowd went home
But the old man still sensed strife,
His final words had touched someone
Who had seen too much of life.

The man approached him quietly,
Stopped a pace or two away,
The blind man said, "Why come to me
When you won't hear what I say?"
He assured him he had listened
"Ah, but did you **hear** one word,
Have you any understanding
Of the changes that occurred?
Strong emotions are life draining,
Fighting users can be too
But they take away your power
When you give up… as you do."

A woman called the man away
And he turned to where she called,
The old man said, "You break my heart,
You're so helplessly enthralled.
You feel like a wooden puppet,
Someone else holds all your strings."
But then he felt a hand take his
And sensed many other things.
Though the helpless trait remained there
There were many strengths there too
And a mound of information
But confusion marred the view.

The old man was quite pleased to find
He could still make a mistake,
That he had not become immune
To the errors others make.

"You take my hand," the blind man said,
"And reveal your true intent,
You're tired of the life you chose
Being drained by sentiment.

Through the eyes of cold emotions
Being kind appears as weak,
Easy fodder for the takers
And the victim users seek.
You possess such depth of knowledge
From experience you've known
But it's all quite disconnected,
You don't see the truth you're shown."

He replied, "I have been waiting
For someone to light the way
To help me walk the path I need
And I found you... here... today.
Would you let me travel with you?
Guide me to a higher plane
So I'll serve some useful purpose
With what life may still remain."

The old man stopped and thought awhile,
He knew something held him here
And the man who stood before him
Did not seem to speak from fear.
"It is not my place to rescue,
All I do is educate...
Though your asking was expected,
We will see if it's too late."
Then he added, "I must warn you,
Your fate will be sealed this night,
Those who use you, will not free you
Without putting up a fight."

The woman called a second time
Quite surprised he hadn't come,
When there had been a test of wills
It was always she who won.

So, she sent for reinforcements,
Those who played his weaknesses,
He would not ignore her wishes,
Her will had to conquer his.
Others came to drag him backwards
Pulling on his 'duty' chain,
To manipulate him, trap him,
With emotion's old refrain.

He responded to their goading
With a smile they didn't know,
Said, "I'm not what you imagine
And it's time for me to go.
I watched you play your silly games
And gained through observation,
But such a place could never be
My chosen destination.
I have courage and a purpose,
Just because my nature's kind
You believe you can control me
But you cannot read my mind!
Feeling drained of life and laughter
Are the wages cowards earn
And I thank you for that lesson
It's a valued one to learn."

The blind man said, "Though that was seen,
Truth is easier to find
If it isn't in a pocket
Scattered somewhere in your mind.
As one piece of information
That you waste time searching for
Will be lost again the moment
You don't need it anymore.
Information forms a circle

Closing of its own accord,
To create a link of knowledge
And that knowledge must be stored.
When the links are joined together
They become a wisdom chain,
Then what you know can't be misplaced
When it's needed once again."
He smiled back in understanding
Knowing that the words were true,
As the old man led the younger
To a clearer point of view.

He had come into the village
To give guidance and support
Did this man have true potential?
He would give the matter thought.
Time provides the information
To those who wait patiently,
"Come walk with me," the blind man said
"And we'll see what we shall see."

*

A step… A tap. A step… A tap,
He'd been waiting for the sound
Of the boy turned into beggar,
And he slowly turned around.

"Master, please, may I come with you?
I won't live long on the street,
When some charity is offered,
I'm too slow… I can't compete."

His companion had stepped forward
Having failed to understand,

"The boy doesn't need assistance,
But like you… a guiding hand."
He told the youth, "Your pace and mine
Will be equal, I suspect,
And your offer to go with us,
I'm delighted to accept."

*

Where at first, they walked beside him
And had tried to talk things through,
As the old man kept his silence
They dropped back a step or two.
They did seem quite strange companions
Yet they bonded instantly,
Mile by mile, revealing aspects
Of their personality.

The dirt road passed through the country
Where the farmers showed delight
In providing food and water
And a shelter for the night.
But once they had left the flat lands
For the barren, rock strewn hill,
The rough ground denied a homestead
Lacking soil that they could till.
With no buildings for night lodgings,
They camped underneath the sky,
And they talked around the fire
As the moon went drifting by.
To their heart-felt conversation
He was paying careful heed,
With his thoughts fixed on which Brother
Was best suited to their need.

On their final night of resting,
The blind man seemed more at ease,
And the boy had felt encouraged
To ask of his memories.

All his sighted years of childhood
Were not ones he would forget,
Having been sold by his parents
As the means to clear their debt.
By the time they had released him,
He was crippled with no sight,
Lost, abandoned on the roadside…
Saved by Brothers of the Light.

"They begin, much like your own youth,
With indentured servitude."
The boy, Tom, said, "Please forgive me,
I did not mean to intrude."
"It's all right," the old man answered
"And I know you've more to ask
But for now, I'll keep my silence,
I must serve my own life's task."
Then the man, whose name was Simon,
Chose to follow the boy's lead,
Saying, "Master, we would serve you,
If you tell us what you need."

"Once again, you show your blindness,
And your need would steal my voice,
It is I who live in service
Giving those I touch… a choice.
You need more than I can give you
And it drains my energy
So, I lead you to my haven
And those far more skilled than me."

They could have no understanding
Of self-knowledge he'd accrued,
To ensure his gift caused no harm
He required solitude.

*

Next day, as they breached a hill top,
A large valley was revealed,
As he led them to the buildings,
Hooded workers tilled the field.
Each one straightened at their passing,
Called a welcome to the three,
The old man said, "We are not blood,
But they are my family."

Brother Stephen, before greeting,
Paused to play his teaching game
As he waited for the blind man
To identify his name.

Laughter made him seem much younger
Than the two thought him to be,
As he called out, "Brother Stephen,
I have brought some friends with me."

Tom was shown his sleeping quarters,
Though the cell seemed quite severe,
The key Brother Anton gave him
Meant more than he could make clear.
As the boy's hand smoothed each surface,
Wonder glistened in his eyes,
Brother Anton eased his struggle
Saying, "I do realise,
You do not need to explain it,

It is written on your face,
In the Brotherhood, we share all,
But we each have our own space."

Simon's room, though somewhat larger,
Held no more than had Tom's own,
But he too appreciated
A place he could be alone.
With their keys tucked in their pockets,
He escorted them to lunch,
Brother Anton said, "Forgive us,
We can be a noisy bunch.
When our Brother ends his travels
We all want to hear his news,
And to add to the excitement
We have you to share your views.
Tell us if we overwhelm you,
It will not be our intent,
Questions show what you require
And will all be kindly meant."

They were cared for... not fussed over,
And at once had felt at ease,
As he added in a whisper,
"Brother Stephen loves to tease.
Your companion will be tested
To discover what he learned,
But their sparring is their pleasure
So, you need not be concerned.
Our blind Brother is an equal,
You will find no pity here,
We just remove the obstacles
So, the path he walks is clear.
That is done through education,
Brother Stephen tests his skill

In removing false impressions
So, his fate he can fulfil."

"Can you tell us how he studied?"
"Was he not blind when he came?"
"Do you know what age he might be?"
"Can you say the blind man's name?"

Brother Anton laughed… but answered,
"When need calls… need finds a way.
Brother William brought him to us,
And his age? I couldn't say.
We give freely of our knowledge
but his name remains unknown,
And we lacked the skills to teach him,
So, the student found his own!

His first teacher saw no reason
Why a blind boy couldn't write
and the boy himself, determined
to not fail through lack of sight.
He pressed too hard on the parchment
And a miracle occurred,
His deft fingers traced a pattern
Which revealed a written word.
Brother William reprimanded
For work done so carelessly,
But was halted in mid-sentence
By his look of ecstasy.
When the blind youth ran his fingers
Over indents far too deep,
He found his own way of reading
And that gift was his to keep.
But as he learned, we learned with him,
Which, to this day, we still do,

We are students here, not masters,
One day, you may teach us too."

*

Freed of kindly inquisition
The blind man sought out his cell
To record that his last journey,
On reflection, had gone well.
His journals, kept beside the desk
Which held treasured gifts within;
As all parchments once thought ruined
Had been set aside for him.

Brother Joseph bound Tom's ankle
Using splints to hold it straight
And assured him, "Being crippled
Does not have to be your fate.
We're a melting pot of knowledge,
It's all here for you to learn,"
And much as the blind man told him
"You become that which you earn."
On his hours freed from study
Tom sought Brother Stephen's side,
To observe the trained stone mason,
Who he hoped would be his guide.

Simon worked with Brother Anton,
Often in the open field,
Slowly learning, that with training,
Raw emotions could be healed.
"When we touch the earth, minds open,
As in caring for the land
It returns to us its blessing
Which in time you'll understand."

When they'd reached the tilled row's ending
Brother Anton said, "Now turn
And admire all your hard work
As the fruits your labours earn."
Simon felt such satisfaction
In the planting he had done
And he reveled in the calmness
Gained from toiling in the sun.

They saw little of the blind man
Who had done all that he could,
They were told, he searched his conscience
To make sure his path was good.

*

Some months later, he was packing,
The road calling once again
Even though, under his armpit
He had felt a twinge of pain.

Simon asked, "Can I go with you,
I could help you find your way?"
But the pain had him distracted
As he answered, "Not today,
I cannot support the burden
Of a single hungry soul,
I must travel unencumbered
If I am to serve my goal."

"Those who fear you might attack you!"
As his purpose, he mistook,
"You should stay here for your safety,
Write your message in a book."

"Those who read don't need my guidance,
Those who can't… have need of me,
How I die is unimportant,
How I lived… will measure me."

Watching on as he departed
Lines of worry left their trace
In a boy's eyes, for a blind man
And what dangers he might face.
As Tom held tightly to his key
Indecision wracked his mind,
Could he forfeit his new safety
To protect a man too kind?

Brother Stephen read his thinking
From his actions… so intense,
"We prepared him for his service,
He is skilled in self-defence.
His white staff may be re-purposed,
As a weapon, should he need,
If some villains seek to harm him
They're unlikely to succeed.
If one here could be called master,
That one Brother would be he,
Growing past his teacher's prowess
As a youth of twenty-three."
His face smiled and his eyes twinkled,
Though he tried to sound quite stern
When he said, "Your teachers wait you,
There is much for you to learn."

*

In a village, at some distance,
On a busy market day,

Noise rolled past, like echoed thunder,
From the crowd who slowed his way.
As he took up his position
Where his voice would be best heard,
Searing pain pushed at his ribcage
Robbing him of breath and word.
His old knees began to fail him,
As he sank down to the stone,
An angel said, "Come, take my hand,
And I'll lead you to your home."

From the crowd stepped forth a woman
Who'd become a trader's wife,
She had recognised the blind man
As the one who'd changed her life.
With assistance from her husband
They helped him into the cart,
Where she settled down beside him
Conscious of his ailing heart.
The herbal potion fed to him
Would be sure to ease his pain,
And she told him, "I'm so grateful
That we get to meet again."

The angel's voice, so pure and clear,
Made him doubt he was alive,
As she said, "Thanks to your teaching
I can live… not just survive.
We are both extremely honoured
By this opportunity
To repay you for your guidance
And your generosity.
When you speak… we often hear you,
Though we need not take your hand,
We can use the skills you taught us

As a means to understand."
Then she laid her head beside his,
Her hand resting on his heart,
When he spoke… with no discomfort
from the rocking of the cart.
"You offer me my life's reward
With your mind so pure and good,
The seed of wisdom has become
Far more than I thought it could."

Word was carried from the village
By those who had called him friend,
To let others know the blind man,
Was approaching his life's end.
By the time they reached his valley
They trailed dozens in their wake
As her voice cried out in anguish
"I have brought him home too late!"

Brother Stephen said, "Please listen,
There is no cause for your tears,
As the blind man was a legend
Having lived past eighty years.
We have twenty travel journals,
All he lived for is not gone,
We pick up his fallen mantle,
So his work will carry on."

Many others came before them
So the Brothers had been warned,
But no word could have prepared them
For the smile his face had formed.

Brother Anton asked the couple,
"If you both would be so kind,

Please relay the conversation…
It's the last one we will find."
The wife said, "I will oblige you
And will try to do my best,
Though he thought I was an angel
Sent to lead him to his rest."
As he listened, Brother Anton
Learned there was more to be found,
As she spoke of their first meeting
Which had turned her life around.

Twenty journals had recorded
What was said to those he'd meet,
With no mention of the outcome…
His reports were incomplete.
Every Brother left their toiling,
Picking up a chalk and slate,
They moved out amongst the mourners
Noting all they would relate.

Through the daylight and the darkness
Many more came down the hill
To pay tribute to the blind man
For his kindness and his skill.

As night wore on, Brother Anton
Found the traders cart once more,
And the man said, "I will tell you
Something you've not heard before.
Though the blind man in his wisdom
Catered for each one in need…
It was not his words that healed me
But his touch!" and some agreed.
"I had lived so full of anger,
I was drowning in my rage,

Through his hand, he took it from me,
And said… Start with a clean page."

Several times before the morning,
Brother Anton heard the same,
He now owned a fuller picture
Of the Brother with no name.

On the hill before the valley,
Rich and poor worked side by side
To construct a mausoleum
Where his body would reside.
Brother Stephen picked his tools up
And he carved into the stone
The words spoken by the angel
Within whom the seed had grown.

Herein lies the un-named blind man,
Healer of those lacking sight
Through his touch and words of wisdom…
A true Brother of the Light.